# DEAD SCALP

## JASPER BARK

Crystal Lake Publishing
Where Stories Come Alive!

www.crystallakepub.com

Join the Crystal Lake community today
on our newsletter and Patreon!
https://linktr.ee/CrystalLakePublishing

Download our latest catalog here:
https://geni.us/CLPCatalog



ISBN: 978-1-968532-01-7

Cover Art: Maarten van Vuuren

Cover Design: Ben Baldwin | benbaldwin.co.uk

Layout: Jacque Day | jacqueday.com



Follow us on Amazon:

# WELCOME
## TO ANOTHER

# CRYSTAL LAKE PUBLISHING
## CREATION

HOWDY PILGRIMS, WELCOME TO THE WILDEST, WEIRDEST PLACE IN THE OLD WEST. THE BLOODY LITTLE BURG OF *DEAD SCALP.*
IF YOU'RE IN TROUBLE WITH THE LAW, IF YOU'RE LOOKING TO DISAPPEAR AND NEVER BE FOUND, THEN ITS DUST CAKED STREETS AND SIN SOAKED SALOONS MIGHT BE THE PERFECT HIDE OUT.
WELCOME TO DEAD SCALP →
JUST BE SURE NEVER TO TRIM YOUR BEARD, CUT YOUR HAIR OR SHAVE YOUR UNMENTIONABLES. BECAUSE IN DEAD SCALP FOLKS ARE MORE AFRAID OF THE BARBER THAN BOOT-HILL! JUST TURN THAT PAGE, IF'N YOU'D CARE TO FIND OUT WHY!

# CHAPTER 1

Clem cleared his throat.

"Y'all have heard the charges agin Charlie McKinnell, made by the Judge—Big Bill."

Big Bill was tall and fat with a streak of meanness longer than his beard. He grunted, warning Clem to move things along.

"Charlie stands accused o' peddling swamp root tonic behind Big Bill's back. Anyone gonna speak for the defense?"

Clem scanned the bar of Big Bill's saloon. Nearly all of Dead Scalp was gathered for Charlie's trial. Not a one of 'em spoke up. They pulled at their beards and stared at the floor, trying not to catch Clem's eye.

All except for Tom Hill, who stepped away from the bar. Nat Mullens put a hand on his shoulder but Tom shrugged it off. "I will."

Bart Sommers, the only man in the room taller, fatter and worse smelling than Big Bill, grabbed Tom by his ginger beard and yanked him forward.

Bart put a cut throat razor to James's beard. "D'you swear by yer whiskers, not to lie nor feed us any bull?"

Tom swallowed. "Sure do."

Bart pushed Tom towards Big Bill and he fell at his feet. Bill leaned forward in his large leather chair.

"The witness has been sworn in," said Clem. "So let's hear his testimony."

Tom got to his feet and cleared his throat. "Well, if it pleases the court."

He glanced nervously at Bill. His expression froze into terror and pain at the deafening discharge of the Colt in Big Bill's hand. A single trickle of blood ran from the hole in Tom's forehead as the back of his head exploded.

"Aww Christ!" Billy Williams jumped with pain as the bullet passed through Tom and clipped his shoulder. Tom's brains dripped from Billy's beard.

Clem raised his eyebrows. "I guess the case for the defense rests."

"Yeah," called a voice from the back. "Rests all over Billy Williams." Everyone laughed, apart from Billy, who scowled and picked the bloody, pink globs from his whiskers.

"Quiet!" roared Big Bill and the laughter died in everyone's throat. "This ain't no laughing matter." The whole bar became solemn as Bart dragged Tom's corpse out back to be burned.

Clem watched Big Bill eye Charlie, a thin, weasley guy with a straggly beard and a lazy eye, who was trussed to a chair in front of Bill. "Ya got anythin' to say 'fore I pass sentence?".

Charlie nodded vigorously. "Damn right I do. How come I'm the only one up here, on trial. What about that bastard Injun, huh?"

Bill scowled "Rivers Flow? Don't worry, I fixed him good."

Big Bill had fixed him alright. Clem had seen to it. He'd ordered the men at the ranch to butcher the Injun's two boys, the ones Rivers Flow had with the young Mexican widow he took in.

Nothing came in or out of Dead Scalp without passing through the old Injun's hands. This was the first time in four decades he'd been caught doing something behind Big Bill's back.

Big Bill needed Rivers Flow alive, but he had to learn he couldn't cross Big Bill. Charlie didn't have a hope.

Charlie continued to whine. "What about Nat then? How come you ain't tried him?"

"Cos Nat admitted everything and you didn't, Charlie. You lied to me. Nat knew the game was up and he came clean. Turned evidence agin you. Told us how the whole set up was your idea."

Charlie struggled and strained to turn his head in Nat's direction. "Why you two faced, son of a rattle snake! Why'd you go and double cross me? You know it wasn't all my idea at all. Lemme outta these ropes and I'll show you whose idea it was. I'll beat the truth outta the rat bastard."

"Already been done."

Nat, a short feller with jet black hair and beard, sunk low in his chair, winced from the bruises he was hiding. He was the only feller in Dead Scalp who looked more weasley than Charlie.

"So that's it then. You're gonna string me up and hang me out to dry, is that it?"

Bill shook his head. "We ain't gonna string you up."

"You're... you're gonna let me go?"

"I'm gonna make an example of you. The court hereby sentences you to death by ingrowing."

Most people caught their breath. Clem had a cold sinking feeling in his gut and the temperature in the bar seemed to plummet.

Charlie's eyes bulged and his jaw dropped. "What? You're joking ain't ya?"

"Do I look as though I'm joking?"

"Look Bill, I fucked up, I admit that. So just hang me, okay. Shoot me, slit my throat if ya must but not that, please... not that."

Bill stood and walked to the bar. "Sorry, Charlie, but I gotta make an example of ya." Bill reached behind the bar and pulled out a pot of glue and Charlie's wanted poster. Clem could see the looks of terror on just about every face in the saloon.

As Bill tacked the poster up, next to the other five behind the bar, Clem took his chance. He walked up to Bill and leaned in. "Are you sure this is for the best, Bill? I mean, you know what happened last time. Is it worth the risk?"

Bill scowled. "Swamp root tonic is our biggest operation, and it's *legit*. I don't care what happened last time. I'm risking a lot more if I don't set a precedent here. Now go hold Charlie's head!"

Clem knew better than to question Bill twice. He walked round back of Charlie and grabbed his head as Bill approached with a razor. Charlie was shaking and fighting his bonds, trying to turn his head away from the razor. "Please Bill, please... it's me... Charlie. How long did we ride together, Bill? Please, just hang me. Hell, I'll even climb up on the scaffold and jump my goddamn self."

Bill took hold of one side of Charlie's mustache and sliced it clean off, making sure to leave no stubble. Charlie let out a shrill scream as the hair came off. Clem hadn't heard anything so high pitched since the little girl whose mother they shot, back in '68. Charlie was jerking his head about so much Bill nearly cut through his top lip taking the other part of the mustache.

"Fuck's sake, Clem," said Bill. Clem just gritted his teeth as Bill returned to the bar, took a big dollop of glue and stuck both sides of the mustache to Charlie's photograph on the wanted poster.

Charlie continued to scream as Bart dragged him off, still tied to the chair. The veins in Charlie's neck were throbbing and his eyes were darting wildly about the room. "For God's sake," somebody shoot me, please just fucking shoot me. Why won't anybody shoot me?"

"Wouldn't make any difference now," Bart disappeared into the back room with him.

The men in the bar got to their feet and started to shuffle out. Nobody caught anyone else's eye. They were all intent on getting home and locking themselves in.

Clem watched Bill as everyone filed out. He stood with his back to them all, staring up at the six posters behind the bar. Each one had a real mustache stuck to it.

# CHAPTER 2

James Briggs wiped the blood from his knife and sheathed it.

The hare at his feet was beginning to shimmer. It was sliced perfectly in half, with all its innards carefully arranged around it. Even the skull was cleaved in two, so you could see its tiny brain.

James thought the shimmer was a heat haze at first, but neither the sunbaked ground, nor the hare's innards, were hot enough to give off such heat. The little pebbles, arranged in arcane symbols around the hare's carcass, began to rattle and shake.

The shimmer got much bigger and moved up into the air above the hare. It hurt James's eyes to look as it rose, like a column, over the hare. As it grew, the shimmering reminded James of long strands of transparent hair, vibrating so fast he couldn't focus on them. He had to keep looking away because his mind couldn't accept what he was seeing.

When the long shimmering strands had risen to about ten feet in the air, they started to part, like a pair of curtains. As they parted they made a shape like a buttonhole. The more James looked at it, the more it reminded him of a pair of cunny lips. James chuckled to himself. *Ain't never been a cunny I wanted to get into this bad,* he thought.

As the center of the shimmering parted further, James could see a place beyond. A place that wasn't anything like the plateau where he stood. James found it easier to look at the place than the shimmering. It was disconcerting.

The shimmering pulled back even more and James could see two figures on horseback waiting in the place beyond. *Must be the welcoming committee.*

One of the guys was real big, with a long black beard and a huge belly. The black mare he rode was doing all it could to bear his weight. The other feller, on a palomino stallion, was shorter and had a thin wiry body, with the longest sandy colored beard James had ever seen. He decided right away that the shorter guy was the more dangerous of the two.

The shorter guy tipped the brim of his hat. "Howdy, you go by the name of James Briggs?"

"Who wants to know?"

"My name's Clem Sorrel, this ornery looking feller here is Bart Sommers. Rivers Flow tells me you're looking for safe passage?"

"Got most of Arizona on my tail. Can't make it to the Mexican border from here, so I need a place to lay low."

"Well we might be able to help you. Course, there's a few things we're gonna need from you first."

"Yeah I heard about that." James reached into the saddle bag at his feet and pulled out a folded sheet of paper. He unfolded it and held it up for Clem and Bart to see. "This here's my 'Wanted' poster, with the five hundred dollar reward and everything. Got my photo on it, right here. Looking real purty ain't I?"

"Tie it round a rock and toss it through the portal here," Clem told him. James complied. Bart caught the package and took the poster off the rock. "I guess it looks like him," he said. "You got the money?"

James held up the saddle bag. "Ten thousand in silver dollars, right here."

"Toss it on through then."

"Reckon I'll just hold onto it till you let me in. Not that I don't trust you fellers or nothing, but I ain't no fool neither."

Clem nodded. "Okay, open up the bag and show us the cash."

James unbuckled the saddle bag and showed them the contents.

Bart squinted. "You reckon that's ten grand?"

"And a little to spare."

James smiled. "Well I reckoned I might need a little spending money."

Bart pointed behind James. "Where's Rivers Flow? I don't see the ol' cuss."

"He went behind that boulder over yonder."

"Why'd he do that?"

"I don't know, you'd have to ask *him*."

Bart ran a hand through his beard. "I don't like it. The Injun usually handles the whole exchange. Why ain't he here to do that?"

Clem was not overly concerned. "The portal's open ain't it? Only Rivers Flow can do that."

"So why did he light out?"

"Considering what we just done to his sons, can you blame him? Would you want to face us after that?"

"He brought that on himself. If he loved those boys so much why'd he give 'em such stupid names?"

"Sun Shines and Grass Grows? Guess he had a sense o' humor."

"Well, I don't like it. 'Less that Injun shows, I ain't lettin' this guy in."

"Why not? He showed us his poster, we know the law's after him. He's got the money. What's the difference?"

"What makes you all fired up to let him in? You know this guy?"

"No, but I'm a little light at the moment. Maybe I could do with the transporter's fee."

"You should spend less time at those card tables."

"Well I'll be sure and take that under consideration. Soon as I get my fee."

"If you lovebirds have finished with your tiff, could you see your way clear to finishing up our little transaction?"

Bart reached for his pistol "You watch your mouth, mister."

Clem put a warning hand on Bart's chest. "Don't be a fool!" He turned back to James. "Portal closes up in a few moments, so you'd be advised to make your way through as best you can. I ought to warn you though. Once you step foot in here, you can't leave, not ever."

"Ain't got nothing holding me here. I'd just as soon never see Arizona again."

He slung the saddle bag over his shoulder and reached out to the edge of the portal. As soon as his hand came into contact with the shimmering, a force shot up his arm and tore through his body. Every part of him vibrated, his muscles spasmed and went into convulsions. He yanked his hand away before he bit his tongue off.

Bart laughed. "Oh yeah, should've mentioned, don't touch the edges none or you'll regret it."

James nodded. "Thanks for the advice." The edges of the portal were beginning to come together and the space James had to get through was getting smaller by the second.

"Best hurry up now. You don't have much time left."

James took a few steps back, then took a running jump at the portal. He leapt, head first at the space between the shimmering columns. It was like jumping between the ripples on the surface of a lake. He cleared the closing portal but his right foot caught the shimmering edge. The intense vibrations tore up his right side and his body jerked violently. He landed badly, still twitching. His left shoulder ached and his chest was bruised from landing on the saddle bag.

Bart laughed as James got to his feet and picked up his saddle bag. The first thing that struck James was how still his new surroundings were. There was no movement of any sort, except for the two men and their horses.

In the plateau James had just left, there had been an intermittent breeze from across the plains. Flies buzzed and birds circled beneath the slow moving clouds. Here the air felt stagnant. James couldn't draw enough breath to fill his lungs. There was no depth of sound. It was like listening underwater. Everything seemed frozen and unending, as though he were in a perpetual dream.

James was just getting used to the new sensations when he heard the click-click of a hammer being pulled back. Bart was holding a pistol on him. It was an old model Colt from around 1860. Everything about the two men was antiquated. Their weapons, their clothes, the way they acted.

"Reckon I'll have that saddle bag," Bart said. He had the drop on James, there was little chance of him missing at this range. James didn't move.

"You can have the ten grand in silver dollars as we agreed."

"Nope, I think I'll take it all. Then leave ya to walk back to town." Bart pointed behind him. "It's two miles south."

"You get a fee for bringing me in, your man Clem just said. You don't need any more from me."

"We got overheads to cover. Your fee just went up. Now hand it over."

James held out the saddle bag with his left arm and slowly approached Bart. When he was four steps away he dropped onto one knee and, using the saddle bag to shield himself, reached for his knife. It was out its sheath and hurtling towards Bart before the galoot had a chance to react.

Bart yelled as the knife went right through his wrist. He let off a shot involuntarily. Blood poured down his hand. Bart's mare panicked at the noise and James took the opportunity to charge him.

James pulled Bart's right foot out of the stirrup and pushed him out of the saddle. Bart swore and hit the dirt. Taking a chance, James rolled under the rearing mare and sprang on Bart, who was lying on his back. He brought his knee down on Bart's chest and was glad to hear a rib crack.

Bart, who stank real bad up close, winced with the pain. He tried a right hook on James who blocked it and pulled the knife out of Bart's wrist. He put the tip of the knife to the corner of Bart's right eye.

James heard another click and felt the cold steel of Clem's rifle barrel at the base of his neck. "Now just a minute there, pardner. We don't look too kindly on killing around these parts. It brings... well let's just call it—unwanted consequences. So why don't you just put that knife away."

"Why don't you put that rifle away?"

"Well now, I'm the one with the drop on you, so I don't reckon you should be telling me what to do."

"No? You're the one told me killing has unwanted consequences. So I don't think you're aiming to shoot. Whereas me, on the other hand, I just had someone try to rob me. So I'm willing to take those consequences if it means keeping my cash. So why don't you lower that rifle and I'll spare this sumbitch's life?"

James felt the rifle barrel leave his neck. He climbed carefully off Bart with his knife held out in front, in case Bart tried something. James grabbed his saddle bag and Bart's pistol. He took the reins of Bart's mare, calmed it and climbed into the saddle. "I ain't the one who's gonna walk back to town. You got a problem with that?"

Clem just smiled. "See you back at town, Bart," he called over his shoulder as he rode off.

"Fuck you." Bart dusted himself down.

"So how long've you been here?" James rode up alongside Clem, scratching his chin. His stubble was growing at a rapid pace.

"Around forty years."

"Forty years, are you sure? You don't look a day over thirty, even with the beard."

"Physically I'm twenty nine, but I've lived for sixty nine years."

"I don't follow you?"

"That's the effect Dead Scalp has. You don't age, you don't fall sick, so long as you ain't fool enough to get yourself killed, you could live forever."

"Forever?

"If you've a mind to."

"Oh, I've a mind to."

"Well you just made an enemy of one o' the most dangerous sumbitches in these parts. I'd be careful I was you."

"He don't scare me. I can handle myself."

"You can handle yourself, I'll give you that."

"So what's with the long beards? Does everyone round these parts have one?"

"Yep, hair's about the only thing that grows here. Don't have no trees, nor plants, all we got's our locks and our beards."

"Well I'm aiming to visit the barber soon as we get to town."

"Don't have no barbers in Dead Scalp. Nobody shaves nor cuts their hair. You'd be advised not to yourself."

"Let me guess, it has certain consequences."

"Damn right."

They came to the head of a bluff. Below them, on a level plain, sat the ramshackle town of Dead Scalp. A rough collection of wooden buildings and unpaved streets.

"So is everyone in Dead Scalp an outlaw?"

Clem led him down a narrow trail to the town below. "Sure do ask a lotta questions don'cha?"

"I'm about to hand over ten thousand dollars for the privilege of livin' here. Reckon I'm entitled to answers."

"Nope, they ain't all outlaws, only half the population's on the run from the law. They got in like you did. As to the rest, we got a lot of whores. Some of those came willingly, others were captured and forced to work in the brothels, bit like the slaves."

"Blacks you mean?"

"Not just the colored folk. We need men who can build and make things, carpenters and smiths. Mostly we kidnap 'em and force 'em to work for us. If they live long enough to work off the ten grand entry fee, we set 'em free."

"You let 'em go home?"

"No, they can't go home. Like I warned you, 'fore you got here, there's no way back. Once you're here, you're here forever."

"So how does a man make a fortune in this town?"

He and Clem reached the end of the trail and approached the first buildings. "There's a few rackets. We always need stuff from the outside. Can't grow shit here, 'cept hair, so we gotta find ways to get food and liquor in without alerting the law."

"I can do that."

Clem steered his horse to one side as they came up to the saloon. James followed him. "Course you gotta give over half of everything you make to Big Bill,."

Clem nodded to two men sitting out front of the saloon. The men nodded to others across the street. James was suddenly aware of at least five men reaching for their weapons.

"Big Bill, he the man runs this place?"

Clem had a broad smile. "Let's just say he's not the man you wanna cross."

James could see five rifles trained on him. He scanned the street looking for routes of escape and froze when he felt a pistol barrel pressed against the base of his spine. Some guy had snuck up behind without James seeing or hearing.

"Speaking of which, I believe you were gonna hand over thirteen grand."

"Agreed price was ten."

"Well I just put it up. You put Bart out of action for at least a month. Big Bill ain't gonna be pleased. Muscle like Bart's hard to come by."

"That don't leave me hardly anything left."

"Been an expensive day for you then."

James handed over the saddle bag and filled his pockets with the coins he had left over. He'd been right about Clem. He was the most   dangerous.

Clem tipped his brim. "Been a pleasure doing business with you,. Now you'll have to excuse me, I got some business to attend to, in a back room."

# CHAPTER 3

Clem needed to get a little drunk before attending to the business. Not so drunk he lost his edge, just enough to hold his nerve.

Doc Hendry let Clem into the back room. Charlie's corpse was laid out naked, on a long wooden table. Clem could see the ingrowing had started. There wasn't a hair left on Charlie's body. All of it had gone, including his beard.

The skin around his chin and scalp was the most raw. It was stretched out of shape by the hair that had forced its way back into his body. Charlie's eyeballs were bugging out of their sockets. Blood was streaming from his ears, his nose, his mouth and asshole. It had pooled around the body and was dripping off the table.

The two slaves in the room were staring at Charlie's body with terror. They were young and new to Dead Scalp. They knew nothing of the ingrowing. That's why they'd been chosen to help with what came next.

Clem fixed 'em with a hard stare. "You boys all right? I don't need to have you beaten or nothing?"

The tallest, a skinny boy with a wispy blond beard took off his hat and gripped the brim. "No, sir, We're fine. It's just, he was screamin' something awful afore we untied him. Then the screamin' kinda choked off and blood started pourin' outta him."

The Doc motioned to the body with his chin. "That's cos all the hair was inside him. First it would've crushed his lungs, then ruptured his internal organs. It's a painful process. This case was kinda fascinating though. Never seen so much hair disappear so quick."

Doc's beady eyes glittered behind his spectacles. He was a short, thin guy, with a bulbous red nose, who came off kinda creepy. Especially when he appeared to relish these details. Clem remembered he'd once been a man of science, back before the drink and the back street abortions put an end to his career. This was just the sort of thing that *would* fascinate them science guys, Clem figured.

Clem addressed the shorter slave. "You get the swamp bark and the matches like I told ya?"

"Yes, sir." He fumbled with a big wooden bowl and dropped the matches. Clem cuffed him hard round the back of the head.

"You drop them matches one more time boy and I'll shoot you, understand? Little slips like that will get us all killed."

The skin over Charlie's belly started to swell and writhe, as though Charlie were pregnant with some hellish beast. Clem felt a sick, nervous feeling in the pit of his gut and wished he was more drunk. "This here's the bit I hate."

Blood began to pour in torrents out of Charlie's ass. Then his stomach sagged and sank back to its normal size as the first hairs poked their way out of his butt.

The hairs acted as if they were alive. They probed the top of the table and the inside of Charlie's thighs. They reared up as if scenting the air and moved towards the edge of the table. Huge wads of hair pushed their way out of Charlie's ass, stretching and splitting the puckered brown skin of his hole.

The hairs grabbed hold of the edge of the table and wrapped themselves around its legs. They moved further abroad, stretching themselves out of Charlie's torn anus and moving across the room. They grasped hold of loose floorboards, doorjambs and window bars. They snaked round the stove in the corner and cottoned on to anything in the room that would give them a purchase.

The slaves backed into one of the only two corners where the hair hadn't fastened itself. Clem and Doc stood in the other.

The taller slave shivered, his voice a sob. "What... what in tarnation is happening? This is unbearable!"

Clem spat on the ground at his feet. "It gets a hell of a lot worse."

Once all the hairs had attached themselves to something, they began to tug at Charlie's asshole. More blood poured out as Charlie's innards were torn from his rectum. Charlie's legs were splayed with the pressure the hair was exerting. They stuck out at right angles to his body. Clem could hear the tendons and muscles in his hips snap and grind as the legs began to move into a more impossible position. Charlie's arms began to move next, reaching straight up, while his shoulders contracted into his body with an awful noise.

Then Charlie's skull collapsed. His face folded into itself, and what was left of his head slithered down the bloody maw that was now his neck. Most of the interior of Charlie's body had been torn out of what had once been his asshole. With one huge, almighty tug the hair turned the rest of his body inside out.

What now lay on the table, was a writhing mass of living hair, ruptured organs and dislocated human bones. The taller slave let out a whimper.

Clem clicked his fingers. "Light that goddamn bark and get over here."

The short slave's fingers shook as he held it over a lit match. "It won't catch. I'm tryin' but it won't catch."

"Hold the match along the edge, not in the middle."

The slave did as he was told and the dried bark finally caught light.

"Now blow out the flame and waft the smoke over that thing's body."

"Why?"

"Don't ask stupid questions, boy, just do as you're told. The smoke from that bark is the only thing that can knock this thing out and keep it under control. But we've got to act quickly, while it's sluggish."

Doc Hendry was filling a big glass syringe with enough strychnine to kill a herd of buffalo, as the slave blew out the flaming bark and edged closer to the thing on the table.

It wasn't as sluggish as Clem thought. The slave didn't see the strands of hair that wrapped themselves around his ankle until his leg was yanked and he toppled to the ground, dropping the bowl with the bark.

More strands of hair caught the bowl and turned it over, trapping the smoke inside. The slave clawed at his throat in desperation as further strands of hair wrapped themselves around it, crushing his larynx and choking him to death.

Clem made a lunge for the bark in the upturned bowl. He didn't see the strands of hair that had pulled the barred grill off the window, until they swung the grill at his head. Bright sparks rattled around Clem's skull as the pain of the impact blinded him.

He may have passed out for a second. He heard breaking glass and guessed the hair was smashing the window with the grill. When he opened his eyes, he saw Doc Hendry make one last attempt to stick the thing with his syringe as it pulled itself out of the broken window.

Doc didn't spot the hair at his feet until it was pulled from under him like a rug. He fell on the tall slave who was curled into a ball in the corner. The Slave gasped when he saw the empty syringe sticking out of his chest.

"Sorry kid," Doc said as the slave frothed at the mouth and went into death spasms.

Clem put his hand to the throbbing lump on his temple and winced. He lay still for a moment contemplating what was worse. What that thing was going to do to Dead Scalp now it was loose, or what Big Bill was going to do to Clem when he found out it had escaped.

# CHAPTER 4

James had been nursing the same glass of whiskey for over an hour. He had to, it cost a damn sight more in Dead Scalp than it did on the outside. But then, everything seemed to cost a damn sight more in Dead Scalp.

Not for the first time that night, he wished he'd taken more silver dollars in the heist. It had been such a risky move. Everyone had said it couldn't be done, that the place had too many men and was too well guarded, but James was desperate, and up against it.

The lawmen had gotten hold of a witness who was willing to testify that James shot Robert Perkins in a card game. Even though Perkins had it coming, John Law had a reason to see James swing.

James's only hope of survival had been Dead Scalp. The lawmen had closed off the border and the net was closing in. He'd heard the rumors about a mystical hideout that the law couldn't touch, the only problem was his lack of the entry fee—ten grand in silver dollars.

So James had staged a desperate robbery. The one theft no one thought possible. James had nothing to lose, so he thought *what the fuck*. It was this or the scaffold.

Looking back he couldn't believe how easy it was. He'd been real careful to stay out of sight when he staked out the old ranch house. Even still, it felt as if the old devil in charge of the place had known he was there.

More than that, it was as if he were purposefully tempting James to come on down and make his move. He left doors unlocked and the gates off the hook. He moved the dogs out of the backyard and he got the guards blind drunk on moonshine.

It looked as though he wanted James to rob the place.

When James had struck, the old devil didn't put up any fight. Not even to save the drunken guards. He just stood by and watched as James blew out their addled brains. When James had put his gun to the old devil's head, he'd shown him exactly where the money was.

James's only mistake was not stealing more saddle bags and more horses. He'd made off to Dead Scalp with as much as he thought he could carry. It had all gone without a hitch.

Well not quite without a hitch. There'd been that slight business at the end, but that didn't matter now. He was here in Dead Scalp and the law could never touch him. He was going to get rich and live forever and that's all that mattered. So long as no one found out, he had nothing to worry about.

James's thoughts were cut short by the sound of feet approaching. He glanced up and saw Clem bearing down on him along with a man who was nearly as tall and fat as Bart. His beard was bigger and he looked about the most dangerous man in a room filled with nothing but dangerous men. He had to be the guy who ran things.

James looked down at his drink and tilted his Stetson so they couldn't see his eyes. He heard them stop at his table. Surely they couldn't have found out already. There was no way that was possible.

A deep, rasping voice. "This him?"

Clem's voice. "Yeah that's him."

"Help you fellers?" James didn't look up.

"I      hear tell you took out one of my men."

"Already paid off that debt."

Bill's voice made James look up with a start. "I'll tell you when you've paid me off. Until then you owe me, understand?"

James blinked. He glanced from Bill to Clem, who had a bruise on his forehead, trying to read their eyes for suspicion. He saw nothing but anger in Bill's eyes but, for a moment, he was sure Clem had seen the fear behind his own. "Reckon I do at that."

Bill wasn't a man you argued with. "Now, Clem here says you can handle yourself and I got something needs handling."

"Any money in it?"

"Let's say you'll be more likely to live if it goes well."

"That ain't the worst offer I've had since I got here."

"Good, you start straight away. Clem'll fill you in on the details."

"So you want me to work for you cos I took out your muscle. That right?"

"No, I want you to help me sort something out, cos you're the new man in town, and that makes you too dumb to realize how scared you oughta be."

Big Bill turned and strode away.

Clem smiled at him. "C'mon, it's already dark and you're not gonna like this."

# CHAPTER 5

Nat was shit faced. What's more, he was up two grand from the poker tables. Life was good.

He'd almost forgotten how bad he felt about Charlie and Tom. He'd done what had to be done though. He'd taken a pretty bad beating from Bill and his men and he had to give someone up. Charlie was the obvious scapegoat. Poor kid always was too trusting.

It was Nat's idea to run a side operation and cut Bill out. Charlie had been real scared of Big Bill discovering their racket. So Nat promised Charlie that he'd take the fall if anything happened. Charlie had bought it too.

The side operation only seemed fair to Nat. After all it had been him and Charlie who'd discovered the miraculous properties of the swamp water.

Charlie knew an old quack who ran a medicine show on the outside. He and Nat had bottled some of the stagnant water from the swamp on the outskirts of Dead Scalp. A sodden and fetid stretch of land next to the graveyard.

The first load of bottles damn near killed anyone who drank 'em. Then someone poured it over their head and discovered it not only cured baldness, but dandruff and head lice too. After that Nat and Charlie couldn't bottle it quick enough.

When Big Bill found out about this, he not only took his cut, but moved in and took over the whole operation. Nat and Charlie were frozen out. So Nat cut a side deal with Rivers Flow to help him move some bottles without Big Bill knowing.

Rivers Flow controlled the traffic in and out of Dead Scalp. He was pissed enough at Bill's high handed ways to go along with it. Then Bill found out what they were pulling, and all three of 'em were in a world of trouble.

Nat never thought Bill would kill Charlie when he sold him out. He felt plenty cut up about it. It was a rotten shame. Charlie had been the only person in the whole of Dead Scalp that Nat gave a shit about. The kid always had a way of getting right under Nat's skin.

Charlie had called Nat two faced. Well he was right. But then, what did he expect? Nat was an outlaw for Christ's sake. People talked about honor among thieves but it didn't mean shit when it came down to it.

Saying one thing to someone, and doing something else behind their back, was what had gotten Nat where he was today. Damn right he was two faced. Two faced and proud of it.

Nat stumbled back towards his lodgings. He was tottering as he entered the dark alley that led to the room where he flopped. He had to prop himself up against the wall and feel his way down the alley.

Nat decided he must be really shit faced. The walls and the ground felt spongy. No, not spongy, soft and fibrous like...like... oh shit!

Strands of hair wrapped themselves tight around Nat's ankles, making it impossible for him to flee. More strands wrapped themselves around his wrists.

"Charlie... Charlie, that you? Oh Christ Charlie, what have they done to you?"

Charlie didn't answer, but Nat felt hundreds and hundreds of individual hairs wrap themselves around the hairs of his head and beard.

"Now listen, Charlie, I know I ratted you out and everything, but honest to God, if I'd known what Big Bill was gonna do to you I never would've said a word." Nat felt more hairs wrap themselves around his own.

"Well okay, I might have said *something*, but I wouldn't have let you take all the blame..."

Nat's words were cut short as the living hairs tugged fiercely at his beard and hair, stretching the skin of his face so taut he could neither blink nor open his mouth to scream with the pain.

Nate saw something glint in the moonlight. It was a shard of glass held by a bunch of hairs. The hairs brought the shard up to Nat's face and buried it in the top of his forehead, just below his hairline.

A sharp, hot agony shot through Nat's face as the hair forced the sharpened glass down, slicing through the skin of his forehead. Then down his nose, through his top and bottom lip and finally over his chin and throat.

Blood streamed from the deep cut in the center of his face. Nat gasped with the shock of the wound, coughing violently as he breathed in the blood.

The other hairs were tugging at his hair and beard. Nat felt the skin of his face peel away from the bones and cartilage of his skull.

As the pain reached a new, burning intensity, more hairs forced themselves through the gap in his face. They wriggled under his skin, scraping it away from the bone as they snaked around his skull. The part of Nat's mind that was still conscious refused to believe that this was happening to him. He couldn't accept that his old friend had become something so monstrous, something capable of doing this to a man. But then, the kid always had a way of getting right under Nat's skin.

The hair wound its way under Nat's scalp and moved further beneath the skin of his neck and over the inside of his shoulders. It scoured the muscle like a thousand white hot filaments.

More hairs bunched up under the skin of Nat's face and tore it away from his skull, stretching it as far as it would go. They burrowed into his eye sockets and wrapped themselves around his eyeballs.

With an insistent tug that sent a shaft of blinding hot pain through his brain, the hairs pulled the eyes from their sockets but kept them behind the eyelids as they folded the torn skin of Nat's face in on itself.

Nat's mind had almost shut down with the torment. His eyeballs were still attached to their optic nerves. They were still sending images to his shrieking brain. It took him a little while to process what he was seeing. But then it dawned on him, as the severed skin and eyeball, from one side of his skull, came face to face with the other.

Charlie had called Nat two faced. He was right, and in the last few moments of his life, both of Nat's faces got to take a good long look at each other.

# CHAPTER 6

"How in hell does this thing move so fast?"

James cantered up to the graveyard next to Clem. He'd been roped into chasing the creature that was once Charlie McKinnel and he'd seen what it had done to Nat Gunderson.

"Damned if I know. Where's the damned thing at? It was headed this way, couldn't have gone anywhere else."

"Why in hell do you have a graveyard anyway? You told me nobody dies here."

"Less they're shot or stabbed or some such."

"And you bury 'em here?"

"No, mainly we burn the corpses so they don't turn out like the thing we're chasing. But we can't burn things like this. The flames just won't take 'em. So we have to bury 'em. For some reason, this land next to the swamp has some kinda power over 'em, keeps 'em dead and buried. We burn the corpses right next to the graveyard for the same reason."

James reined in his horse at the rough stone entrance. The land next to the swamp was damp and oppressive. The place felt old and very, very dead. "So you've had this happen before? I mean, you've shaved some poor fucker's beard off and they've turned into one of these things?"

"Only when Big Bill really wanted to punish someone. And we've never had one get away before. They're usually easy to handle, so long as we burn the swamp bark to knock 'em out."

"How many times have you done this?"

"Seen the posters behind the bar?"

"Ones with the mustaches stuck to 'em?"

"That's right, there's your answer."

Doc Hendry rode up behind them. "Has it got here yet?"

Clem peered through the waning light. "Can't see it."

Doc Hendry dismounted, lit the kerosene lamp from his saddle and peered through the entrance. "You ain't seen it cos you weren't looking in the right place."

"What do you mean?"

"Look, right here." The Doc raised his lamp. James and Clem dismounted and joined him at the entrance. Doc pointed to the center of the graveyard.

Between the graves they saw what looked like some kind of twisted plant. As they peered closer, they realized it was the strange hair creature. It had somehow bedded itself into the damp soil of the graveyard. It looked like a giant clump of twisted flesh covered in impossibly long strands of hair. The hair was snaking between the graves, as if it had a mind of its own.

James suppressed a shudder. "What in God's name is it doing? Is this normal?"

Clem spat on the wet ground. "Nothing about these things is normal. But I ain't never seen one do this before. Let's light up a bunch of swamp bark and take a closer look."

James watched Clem and Doc light their bark, then blow out the flames, so it smoked. He wasn't certain how the bark knocked out these monsters, but he followed suit. Each of them held the bark in front of them as they entered the graveyard. The ground was soft, mossy and damp, water soaked into James's boots.

The first thing he noticed was that there were eleven graves. "Hey," he said. "There are only six posters behind the bar, but there are eleven graves here."

Clem looked at James like he was an idiot. "Think we were the first people to live here?"

"There were others before you?"

Clem didn't answer. But he did put his arm up to stop James from moving forward. Clem pointed at the ground. James looked down and saw hair stroking the front of his boot. Clem removed his arm and James slowly moved his foot back.

Was that fear on Clem's face? "This thing is more dangerous than you can believe."

"I already seen what it can do."

"You ain't seen shit, boy."

Doc raised his lantern. The thing was sinking further and further into the ground, burying itself in the soft, spongy earth. The body beneath all the hair started to ripple, waves were passing through it. Then it started to go into convulsions, something shot out and flew at least fifteen feet up in the air.

James jumped back and dropped his smoking bark. It landed next to the ends of some hair and they withdrew from the bark, pulling themselves rapidly backwards. *So the bark does have an effect on these things*, James thought.

James heard a wet thud behind them as he was picking up his bark. He spun round and saw something burrow its way into one of the graves. The hair thing had another convulsion and something else shot from under its hair.

James took a step back onto one of the graves and craned his neck, trying to see what had shot out of the thing. Something warm hit him in the forehead with a wet slap. He jumped and pulled the hot, slimy thing from his face.

It looked like a ruptured human liver, with living hairs growing out of it. The liver wriggled in his fingers and he threw it at the ground in disgust. The organ crawled onto the grave at James's feet and started to dig its way into the soil.

Clem pointed at it. "The hell is that?"

James thought that obvious. "A liver with hairs. It's digging its way into this grave."

The liver had almost disappeared by the time Clem and Doc joined James at the grave to have a look.

Doc scratched at the back of his neck. "I'll be darned,"

They turned to look back at the thing as it convulsed once again and shot something else into the air.

Doc followed the trajectory of the object and watched as it hit another grave.

Clem craned his neck. "What is it, Doc?"

"Looks like a busted lung covered in hair. It's burying itself in this here grave."

James reached for his pistol. "What the hell is going on?"

Clem put a warning hand on his wrist. "Fucked if I know."

All three of them backed towards the entrance and watched as the hair thing shot eight more hair covered organs into the air. Each of them landed on a grave and dug itself in.

Clem scratched at his beard. "Any idea what's going on, Doc?"

"Well, I ain't certain, but my guess is it's sporing."

"Sporing! What in hell does that mean?"

"It's what fungi do when they want to reproduce. They shoot hundreds of spores up into the air, hoping they'll land on a cow pat, or a rotting tree or whatever they grow on. I read a paper on it once, many years ago."

"I ain't ever read anything like that in the paper."

"This was a scientific paper."

Cogs turned in James' brain. "That thing's trying to reproduce? Ya mean it's trying to have sex with the other corpses?"

"I was just hypothesizing."

"Hypothe-what?"

"I was throwing ideas out. It reminded me of the paper I read on fungus spores is all."

James felt the ground shudder. They all turned to look at the thing, which was sinking into the sodden ground, dragging all its hair after it. Finally it sank from sight and there was no trace of it left.

Clem and Doc started to walk back into the graveyard, being very careful about where they trod. James followed them. When they got to the spot where the thing had bedded in, they found a mound of freshly moved earth and nothing else.

Clem fixed Doc and James with a mean look. "Well that saved us a whole heap of trouble. As far as Big Bill's concerned we dealt with this business and that thing is now good and buried in this graveyard, understand?"

Doc looked relieved. "Fine by me."

James shrugged. "I got no arguments,."

"Good, now let's get the hell outta here. I got whores to fuck and whiskey to drink."

James followed Doc and Clem out of the graveyard. Then he jumped in his saddle and rode back into town.

# CHAPTER 7

It was getting close to dawn when Bart rode up to the graveyard dragging the corpse of the woman behind him. He had to butcher and burn the bitch himself now he'd fallen out of favor with Bill.

In the past, Bill would have sent one of his lackeys to dismember and burn the body. Bart hardly ever came out here, to this desolate spot by the graveyard. He'd sent more than a few bodies though, and more than a few lackeys. It wasn't usually whores that Bart murdered. Mostly it was guys that got in his way or looked at him wrong.

Bill had always turned a blind eye to his murderous rage, cos Bart was useful to him. Besides, it made men more afraid of Bart, and that made them more afraid of Bill, knowing he had a mad dog on a leash.

That was before James had sideswiped him, that sneaky little shit. Bart had limped back into town with a bruised shoulder, busted ribs and a wounded hand starting to go bad. Doc Hendry had fixed him best he could, but Bill wouldn't see him.

He was out in the cold for the time being. But that would change. James might think he had everyone fooled but Bart knew better. He might have wrangled his way into Bill's good books, trying to replace Bart, but he'd get the goods on him soon. There was something about James that wasn't right, and when Bart found out what it was, he was gonna fix him good. He'd make James wish he'd never set foot in Dead Scalp.

Bart had been drinking while Clem and James were out chasing whatever Charlie McKinnell had become. If Bart had been in charge, the thing would never have escaped. Clem was slipping and James couldn't be trusted. Bill would find out, soon enough.

After he'd got good and drunk, Bart had gone round to Molly's brothel. Bart liked to break in the new girls, let 'em know what they could expect from now on. Many of 'em had been snatched from regular life and had never even sucked a dick before, let alone worked in a brothel.

Some of 'em were married, others even had jobs, like being a librarian or a school teacher. Bart couldn't believe how bad things were getting on the outside if they were letting women have jobs. There were some real uppity bitches among 'em. They'd put on all kinds of airs, making threats about what was going to happen when their disappearance was discovered.

No-one was coming for 'em though, they'd find out pretty soon. They'd never be found in Dead Scalp. They were gonna be whores for the rest of their lives, and if they didn't get themselves killed, those lives were gonna last longer than most.

Molly let Bart break 'em in for free. By the time he'd finished with 'em, they had a pretty good idea of what they had to look forward to. He enjoyed the ones who were full of fire and defiance at the beginning. By the time he was finished with 'em, they broke down and let him do whatever he wanted.

Bart had a talent for taming the bitches. He knew exactly how to find the source of their strength and self-worth. Then he wouldn't just take it away from 'em. He'd destroy it utterly. After that you had a whore you could do pretty much anything you wanted with.

Bart had learned how to do this from his mother of all people. She'd raised him by herself and she had a way of honing straight in on a man's weakness. She'd done as much with Bart.

She'd never chided him for all the trouble he'd caused. Instead she'd pitied him his sinful ways. It cut Bart to his very core that the things that caused the other kids to fear him, brought only pity from his mother.

She knew this, and she used it remorselessly. Made him feel small and insignificant, a failure she looked down on. He grew to hate that pity and fear it. Fear it in his mother and any other person he came across.

That's how Bart had turned out the way he did. He made people fear him, hate him and respect him, but he wouldn't tolerate pity in anyone. That's why he was so good at breaking the bitches in. He was paying each and every one of them back for the pity his mother had terrorized him with.

When he'd called at the brothel, Molly wouldn't let him have a girl for free. She'd greeted him personally and given him a bottle on the house, the real stuff too, not the watered down shit she gave to most customers. Then she'd explained to him, as sweetly as she could, that according to Bill's orders, Bart wasn't to get no more free pussy from now on.

Bart was close to beating her unconscious, but Molly knew her way around him. She assured him it was only temporary, that he'd be back in with Bill in no time, and then she'd make certain to do something real special for him. But she had to ask him to pay just this once, cos she couldn't afford to get on the wrong side of Bill.

Bart had thrown his coins on the floor to make certain Molly got down at his feet to pick the money up. Then he'd staggered into the dark room where the new arrival was chained to the wall.

Straight away she started into him. Calling him a filthy pig who stank. Telling him that nothing in the world would make her submit to his lustful demands. He smacked her around a little. Nothing that would break bones or knock her unconscious, just enough to make her see sense.

That didn't do a thing to shut her up. She started screaming and calling him names. Asking him if this was the sort of man he was? The sort who had to beat a woman senseless before she'd sleep with him.

Bart could see a more brutal approach was needed, so he pulled out his knife and put it to her throat, hard enough to draw blood.

Then he pulled his cock out. She looked down at his stiff cock, swollen with blood, and she laughed. A bitter mocking laugh that made him wilt.

"Call that a cock?" she said. "My two year old boy has a bigger cock than that. You think I'm going to be scared of something that tiny?"

Bart really lost his temper then. It was one insult too many. He'd been in enough bath houses to know he was fairly well hung.

He couldn't take any more. He'd been forced to pay for his cunny. He'd been frozen out by Big Bill. And he'd been blindsided by that little pissant James Briggs. There was only so much humiliation a man could take.

So he took the knife and sliced through the bodice of her dress. Then he tore the material apart and sliced the straps on her brassiere. "Go on, take a good look you pig," she'd said as her breasts swung free.

Instead of touching her breasts and letting her mock him some more, he stuck the knife in the side of her body. She wailed in pain and outrage. Then she spat in his face and called him a worm. A tiny little worm who needs a knife to feel big.

Bart was filled with a blinding fury. He couldn't find her weak spot. Couldn't pin down what gave her such strength and self-worth.

He stuck the knife in her stomach. She wailed again, even louder and this got Bart good and hard. Before she could spit at him, Bart pushed his cock into the bleeding gash in her stomach.

Her stomach wall gripped his dick tight. He liked the way her blood felt dripping off his balls. He even liked the way her innards parted as he pushed his cock into 'em. But he hated the way she'd stared at him the whole time he was doing it.

Her stare spoiled the whole thing. He was fucking her to death, but he didn't feel at all powerful. She was dying, but her sneer had made him feel small and pathetic. He took his knife and stabbed it in her jugular, then sliced down the vein.

The blood sprayed both of them. A fierce jet that left him dripping with gore. The look on her face as she died had made his cock shrink. It wasn't the contempt that shone in her eyes as she died, it was the pity that cut him to his core.

In her dying moments the woman had pitied Bart. Pitied him worse than his mother ever had. Bart's cock shriveled quicker than if he'd been standing in a snow drift. It plopped out of her stomach and retreated up into his wrinkled ball sack till it was smaller than Bart had ever seen it.

At this point Molly walked in. Bart was actually crying as she entered. Tears ran down his cheeks and blood dripped from his tiny little dick. He knew, in that moment, that she no longer feared him. That he would never have power over her again. Not after she'd seen him like this.

"Bart honey, you best take that body up by the graveyard and burn it," Molly said. Bart nodded meekly. Then Molly unlocked the shackles and Bart dragged the body outside as if Big Bill himself had ordered it.

Bart tied the woman's ankles with rope, then fastened her to the saddle of the nag he kept as back up. Then he'd ridden off, dragging her bloodied corpse behind him.

Her body was beaten up by the time he got to the graveyard. In the dawn light he could see that, in spite of the damage the ride had done to her face, she was still looking at him with awful pity.

Bart climbed down from his nag and untied the rope from the horn of his saddle. He dragged the corpse up the tiny hillock next to the graveyard; the only spot of dry ground close enough to the graveyard to burn a body.

Bill walked over to the woodpile that was supposed to be stocked for just this sort of occasion. There was a tiny collection of logs and an even smaller pile of kindling. A half empty kerosene bottle sat next to the wood. Hardly enough to set light to a corpse.

Bart cursed his bad luck. Things were getting scarce in Dead Scalp lately. Surely Bill must know about this. How could he let stocks get so low? How could Bill let little shits like James steal Bart's place in his favor?

Bart began to build a fire as best he could. He glanced on over at the graveyard. It looked kinda different. As if it had changed color.

Then it struck Bart. He knew what was wrong. There was a brown carpet growing across the whole graveyard and out of the gates.

It looked like very fine brown grass sprouting up out of the ground. Bart blinked and looked again. That couldn't be right. No grass grew in Dead Scalp. Yet more and more of it was appearing all the time. It advanced up to the little hillock where Bart stood. Then he realized that it wasn't grass. It was hair!

Within seconds, hair started to sprout from the ground beneath Bart's feet. He dropped the wood and forgot about burning the woman's body. Bart ran for his horse as the ground all around him grew hair.

Before he could get to the nag, the hair at his feet wrapped itself around his ankles. Bart was held fast. He tried pulling with his legs and tearing at the hair with his hands, but he was unable to raise either of his feet.

For the first time in forty years, Bart was suddenly very scared. He didn't recognize the feeling at first. It crept into his gut like a chill weight. His chest rose and fell with heavy, convulsive breaths. Then Bart noticed how much he was sweating and it suddenly hit him. He was more scared than he'd been as a boy, when his mother had fixed him with her eye and he knew she was going to skewer him with her ice cold pity.

Bart had forgotten about fear since he came to Dead Scalp. He was the baddest bastard, in a magic town, where you never got old or died. He'd had nothing to be afraid of, until this very moment, when there was a sudden and growing likelihood of his death.

The hair sprouting from the ground wove its way up his legs and fastened onto his waist, unbuckled his belt and tugged his trousers to the ground.

"Mother fucker!" Bart shouted and grabbed at his pants, but they disappeared beneath the morass of hair that was surrounding him. The hair began to bind itself to his legs and hundreds of individual hairs wrapped themselves around Bart's leg hairs.

The hair worked its way up his legs from ankles to thighs. Bart winced as each leg hair was yanked, sending tiny pin pricks of pain up both his limbs. Bart glanced over at the corpse of the woman. The look of pity that was seared into her features seemed to have intensified and he saw his mother gazing out at him from her face.

Hair sprung up from the ground all around her. It folded itself over her limbs with a gentleness that could almost be mistaken for love. It rolled under her still form like a canopy and lifted her body from the ground.

Bart watched as the woman's body was passed along the carpet of hair on a single ripple that moved from strand to strand and carried her back towards the graveyard. Bart saw that the graveyard, and the ground that surrounded it, were now covered with a luxurious lawn of hair. The lawn was spreading quickly and Bart could see it wouldn't be long before it reached the town. *God help those bastards when it hits*, hc thought.

That brought him back to his own predicament. The hair growing over his legs had reached his crotch and begun to fasten onto his pubic hair. First the hairs around his scrotum, then around his anus, finally the bush above his cock.

Every attempt Bart made to stop the hair's progress brought him more torment. The hair pulled on the follicles and refused to let go, no matter how desperately he clawed.

The strands with a tight hold of his short and curlies began to retreat back into the ground. Bart was pulled into a squat. His crotch throbbed with the pressure the hair was exerting.

The agony was so great he hadn't even noticed the hair that had crept under his shirt and taken hold of the hairs up his back. He wasn't aware it was even there until it began to pull him backwards, and away from the hairs that were tugging at his crotch. By then it was too late.

Bart screamed and cussed in anger and pain. Tore at the hair coming out of the ground around him, like a foul mouthed toddler trying to pull up grass. He was as helpless as a squalling infant in the hands of a parent who means to teach it a lesson.

For a moment this scared Bart more than the damage the hair was doing to his body. Then a deeper, fiery pain burst from the skin around his crotch. It wasn't until Bart heard the rending and smelled the blood gushing down the insides of his thighs, that he looked down and saw the skin above his bush had torn and was coming away from his body.

Bart suddenly felt very cold and his mind disconnected itself from what was happening to him. The disbelief cushioned him from the shock of what was being done to his body. The tear in his skin widened and travelled along the sides of his scrotum then around the back of it.

The full extent of what was occurring only hit Bart when he watched the base of his foreskin fold over on itself and peel away from his penis, like the sleeve of a sweater turned inside out. The pink erectile tissue and the bright red glans beneath looked so delicate and fragile that Bart sobbed with pity for his cock. Then despised himself for feeling the one emotion he hated most of all.

Bart's scrotum detached itself and his testicles plopped out. Two pink and white ovals dangling from red and brown, tubular ducts. The inside of his dick looked soft and moist in the dawn light. More hairs wrapped themselves around what was left of Bart's reproductive organs and yanked them so hard they ruptured and tore away from his body.

Bart howled with rage and anguish as blood flooded from his loins and pooled beneath him. He was livid about everything that had been taken from him. Since Charlie McKinnell's death, the hair had taken his income, his power, and now his manhood.

The hair had known exactly how to find the source of his strength and self-worth. But it hadn't just taken it from him. The hair had destroyed it utterly.

Bart just hoped he bled out before anyone found him. If they did find him alive, they'd have a man you could do pretty much anything they wanted with. Except pity him. Dear God don't let them pity him.

# CHAPTER 8

James woke slowly. He'd drunk himself to sleep the night before, and he was wary of the hangover that might be waiting when he opened his eyes.

He'd needed the alcohol to wash away what he'd seen last night. Like the mess that was left of Nat Gunderson. Or the strange hair creature trying to pollinate the graveyard with its ruptured organs, before it buried itself.

The way Clem had told the story, Big Bill had been pleased with all of them. So pleased, he gave James a night's lodgings in the saloon, and a frec whore, who James was too drunk to use in the end. He could have made use of her now, if he didn't have such a splitting head.

James pulled back the cover and climbed off the horse hair mattress. *Horse hair*, he thought, and shuddered. He walked to the dresser at the foot of the bed, leaned over the earthenware bowl there, and poured a whole pitcher of water over his head.

This helped clear his head, but it didn't do anything to stop the pounding. He stared in the cracked mirror and stroked his chin.

After one day here, he had a full grown beard and his hair was longer too.

That's when he heard the first scream. It was high pitched and hysterical. Probably a woman's scream, but James had heard men make similar noises in his time. It had come from the street.

James pulled on his pants and walked through the saloon to see what the commotion was. What he saw made his stomach lurch and sweat break out on the back of his neck.

All along the street hair was growing out of the ground, like a fine brown carpet or an auburn lawn. It was creeping up the sides of buildings like vines and breaking through the walls. Many of the people on the street were stuck fast to the ground. The hair had grown over their feet and around their ankles and was holding them tight.

James saw two women fighting over a ladder that could have led them both to safety, if they'd helped each other, as long strands of hair reached up from the ground and engulfed them both. He saw a man clubbing a horse till he drew blood, as the trapped horse whinnied and bucked in desperation at the hair that was wrapping itself around its legs.

Doc Hendry was trying to make his way to the saloon. He was holding the tiny lump of swamp bark that he had from last night. Great clumps of hair were rising up all around him like brown, fibrous waves. Doc would wave the smoking bark at one clump, to ward it off, and another clump would loom ominously over him.

Doc would then have to fend that clump off while the first closed in on him.

He was within ten feet of the saloon when an unseen clump grabbed him round the middle like a tentacle and lifted him off his feet. Doc yelled and dropped the bark. The tentacle dragged him under an ocean of undulating hair.

"Let go of my fucking leg!" James heard a familiar voice growl. He turned to see Big Bill and Clem advancing through the hair towards the saloon. They were both carrying Civil War sabers. They used them to hack at the surrounding hair like machetes slicing through foliage. As each new tendril of hair reared up over them they attacked it with the blade.

A woman had hold of Big Bill's legs. Great lengths of hair had wrapped themselves around her legs and waist. She was lying prostrate and her fingers dug into Bill's leg. Her face was etched with terror and pleas for help.

"I said let go!" Bill snarled. He brought his saber down on her forearms, severing them just below the elbow. The woman screamed as the hair dragged her into its seething undergrowth. Within seconds, all that could be seen of her were the stumps of her arms, spraying the hair red with blood.

Bill reached the steps of the saloon. As he was mounting them a tendril of hair seized his right wrist preventing him from wielding the saber. Another tendril grasped his left shoulder and began to tug him back.

James rushed from the doorway and snatched the saber from Bill's hand. He chopped at the hair that held Bill prone. It was tougher than it looked and the saber's blade was chipped from severing the woman's arms. Finally James hacked his way through the hair. "About fucking time," Bill said as the hair fell from his wrist and shoulder.

James ran up the steps after Clem and Bill. Before he could get back into the saloon he heard a thump behind him. He turned to see Doc Hendry standing on the top step. The skin of Doc's hands and face seemed stretched and misshapen, as though something was writhing beneath it.

Blood trickled from Doc's nostril and the corner of his mouth. His eyes were filled with an inexpressible pain and his movements were strange and jerky, as if he weren't in control of his body. Between Doc's legs, James caught sight of a thick cable of hair that appeared to be fixed to his back. James's mouth went dry as he realized that the hair had torn a hole in Doc's back and forced its way beneath his skin while he was still alive. It was using Doc as a living meat puppet.

Before James could say anything, Clem moved towards Doc to help him. Doc's head jerked backwards and there was an audible click as his jaw dislocated and his mouth opened impossibly wide.

Clem froze as he realized something was wrong. Hair streamed out of Doc's mouth, dripping with Doc's blood and saliva. It latched onto Clem's own hair and entwined itself inextricably about it. The cable of hair at the back of Doc began to retreat, taking Doc and Clem with it.

Clem cried out and stumbled forward, trying to dig his heels in and pull himself free. James caught hold of Clem's waist while Big Bill grabbed his shoulders. "Get it off, get it off," Clem screamed and hacked at the hair with his saber.

"You can't cut your hair, that'll kill you," said Bill, reaching into his boot for a knife. Bill took hold of Clem's chin and put the blade against the top of his forehead. James watched in horror as Bill cut into the skin and sliced along Clem's hairline. Clem yelled with pain as a thick veil of blood spilled over his face. Bill continued to cut along the hairline, moving the knife around the back of Clem's head, then up the other side of his face and over the top of his ear.

The scalp started to peel away from the top of Clem's skull. Bill didn't need to cut through the last of it. It was torn from Clem's head as the hair from Doc's mouth shot back into his head. The hair yanked Doc's body from the top step and engulfed it once again. James, Clem and Bill fell backwards through the door of the saloon. "Get him up to my office," Bill ordered as he got to his feet and stomped up the stairs.

Clem was twitching with shock as James lifted and dragged him towards the stairs. Clem's face was covered with a layer of blood so thick, James could only see the whites of his eyes and his bared teeth. The blood was starting to clot around the frayed edges of skin that clung to Clem's temples. James could see the white of Clem's skull beneath the gore that speckled it.

James dragged Clem up the stairs and through the door of Bill's office. Bill locked and bolted the door behind them and closed all the shutters on the windows. James laid Clem down on a couch; he appeared to be unconscious.

Bill was seething. "I thought you said you sorted this thing out."

"We did."

"So why's my town covered in hair? Didn't you bury that thing properly?"

"Well, it kinda buried itself."

"What do you mean?"

"It was stuck in the ground of the graveyard when we found it. Then it started shooting its innards up into the air. The innards were covered in hair and they landed on the other graves and buried themselves. Doc Hendry said it was sporing, like a mushroom. Then it just sunk into the ground and disappeared."

Bill shook his head in disgust and disbelief. "I oughta kill both of you."

"Can't we just burn some of the swamp bark and drive all the hair back?"

Bill knelt in front of his safe and unlocked it. He removed a small burlap sack and emptied its contents on his desk. Twelve small pieces of bark sat on the desktop. "That's all the bark we have left. We've scraped every last piece of it off of the dead trees in the swamp, and that's all we have left."

"How come?"

"Cos nothing grows in this godforsaken place, that's how come. Nothing 'cept hair. Think we're gonna drive that murderous tide of hair back with just this?"

"No."

"Exactly."

Clem came round with a groan.

Bill shouted at him. "You fucked up, Clem! You fucked up and look how things turned out. This isn't right, it isn't right. It shouldn't be happening. I had assurances. You remember? Assurances! This place is mine now. Mine! As long as the sun shines, the grass grows and the rivers flow. That's what I was promised!"

Bill paced the floor of his office, tugging at his beard in thought. James knew enough to keep his mouth shut while Bill ruminated. "This is Tsiishch'ili's doing I'll swear it is. It's got his name written all over it. If I could put my hands round his stinking throat all over again... Wait, that's it... I'll summon up the conniving redskin, that's what I'll do. I've still got all the stuff to do it."

He turned to James. "You look after Clem. I've just got to go get some stuff from the other room. Don't let anyone in till I get back." With that, Bill left by a connecting door.

Clem groaned again, and his eyelids fluttered. James shook him to keep him conscious. "Clem, stay with me, Clem. What was Big

Bill talking about? Is this place really his? What did he mean he had assurances?"

Clem licked his lips with a dry tongue. His breathing was little more than a rasp. "There's some whiskey in the bottom drawer of Bill's desk," he said. "Real good stuff, single malt, bring it to me."

"Won't Bill be mad?"

"Think I give a fuck what Bill thinks? Fetch me that whiskey and I'll explain everything."

James got the whiskey from the bottom drawer and Clem took a good long pull on the bottle. He sighed and wiped some of the blood from his eyes. "What Bill means is that he had assurances from the Injuns who were here before us."

"This place used to belong to the redskins?"

"Whole damn country used to belong to the redskins."

# CHAPTER 9

Clem was sorry he'd come to. It was more painful to be conscious. The top of his head stung like a motherfucker. A throbbing sting that grew in intensity. Just when he thought he could bear it, the pain got worse.

The whiskey he was swallowing would have tasted a whole lot better without all the blood in his mouth. Even still, it helped with the pain.

James was asking him all kinds of fool questions about Bill's outburst. Something about James didn't sit right. Clem had been aware of this for a while. It was the money that tipped him off. James had fought like hell to stop Bart taking the silver dollars off him, but then he'd handed them over meekly when Clem and the others got the drop on him. It was almost as if he didn't think the money belonged to him. Clem had come to suspect he should have listened to Bart before he let James in.

None of that mattered now. Clem was going to die soon. If not from the scalping, then from the monstrous hair that was tearing down the town. James was the closest thing he had to a confessor.

"This is a sacred place to the Navajos. A secret they kept for centuries. In fact most of *them* don't even know about it. We only learned about it by accident. We were on the run from the law at the time."

"You and Bill?"

"And the other members of the Baldwin Gang. Named after Bill, that's his name, William Baldwin. Wasn't Bill put the gang together, that was Edward Davies. Bill took over after Ed got his fool head blown off, second time we robbed a train. We did pretty good for a while. Made a lot of money and spread a lot of money around. That way no one went blabbing to the law and we always had a place to hide.

"Problem started when we robbed a train with federal wages. Thought we'd hit the jackpot. Then we discovered we'd stolen a military payroll. They weren't gonna rest till every member of the gang was swinging from a scaffold. Right alongside everyone who ever helped us. We soon ran out of places to hide.

"We split up to avoid detection and they picked us off, one by one. Me and Bill ended up hiding out in the wilds, living off whatever we could kill and nearly starving as a result. We was stalking this hare when we saw this young Injun shoot and make off with it. We followed him, meaning to kill him and take back the hare.

"He led us to this hidden plateau, where this ol' Injun was waiting for him. We thought we'd wait while they skinned and cooked the hare for us, then we'd kill 'em. But instead of cooking the hare they performed this weird ceremony and opened up a sort of shimmering gateway in thin air. We couldn't believe what we was seeing. It didn't make any sense, it was almost as if we couldn't look at it without losing a part of our minds. You probably had the same feeling when *you* saw it.

"Then we saw the ol' Injun passing stuff back and forth with other Injuns who lived inside the gateway. Eventually the shimmering gateway started to get smaller and then it just disappeared. After that they cleared everything away and burned the hare. While they was doing that, we lay in wait and ambushed 'em as they left.

"We beat on 'em a little, to get 'em to tell us what they was doing, but they refused. They was only an old man and a young boy, but they stood up to some rough treatment. Finally we roasted the ol' Injun's feet over a fire till he gave in.

"The old bastard told us he was opening a portal to a magical realm that existed outside of time and space. He called it the Eternal Dreaming. It was part of the place that our souls go to when we dream. It had been cultivated by the Navajos like the maize that they grew. They'd coaxed it into being a tiny bit at a time, building a living space out of tiny bits of dream, knitted together over generations till they had a whole realm. That's why nothing grows here, it's not part of the normal world."

"What about the hair that grows here?"

"The Navajos believe that a man's hair is the physical manifestation of his dreams. That's what the ol' Injun told us. I remember an

Injun scout we had back in the war, refused to cut his hair because he'd lose his edge if he did. Said it sharpened his intuition. It was his dreams you see, spilling out of his scalp, day by day. In a land made up of dreams, hair's the only thing that's gonna grow."

"Maybe, I dunno."

"You don't know shit. You wanna hear this story or not?"

"Okay, calm down."

"So this Eternal Dreaming is a place where their ancestors live for all eternity. Only the wisest and most pure of their medicine men and women were chosen to live there. They would pass over before they died and stay there forever more, without ever aging, getting sick or dying. The ol' Injun's family had been tending to the needs of their ancestors for generations. His bloodline was part of the magic that anchored the place to this world. The care and tending of the Eternal Dreaming was passed on from parent to child throughout the ages.

"Course, soon as we heard about this place, where you never got old and died, where the law couldn't touch you, we knew we had to get in there. So we tortured them both till they opened the portal for us. Then we put a knife to their throats and threatened to kill the boy and the ol' Injun' if the ancestors didn't let us pass through the portal.

"They tried to warn us off, telling us that once we stepped through we could never leave, but we didn't pay no heed to that.

See, they knew that if the boy and the ol' Injun    died, then they'd lose their anchor to this world, so they had to let us in.

"I held a knife to the ol' Injun's neck while Big Bill jumped through the weird shimmering hole between this place and the outside. Then he threatened to scalp the head ancestor, an old Navajo called Tsiishch'ili, if they didn't let me in. I jumped over as it was closing up. Nearly didn't get my foot through. Got a helluva shock, just like you.

"Once we were inside we took a look around and decided the place was a goldmine waiting to happen. It was the perfect hideout. We could charge huge amounts of money to outlaws who wanted to avoid the law and live forever. We could even run rackets on the outside without fear of getting caught. All we had to do was tidy the place up a bit, make it fit for proper white folks, and get rid of the Injuns that were living there.

"They'd avoided us ever since we arrived. Being all mystic and such, they weren't violent like us, and they were much older. We knew they were plotting to get rid of us, so we struck before they got a chance to do anything.

"We rounded 'em all up and told 'em we were taking over. Then we forced 'em to tell us how the place worked and what we needed to do to control it. We tied 'em all up and started torturing 'em. We scalped the first couple we went to work on. Thing was, they almost seemed relieved that we took their whole scalps off and not just their hair. They seemed terrified of cutting their hair.

"So the next thing we did was shave a couple of their heads. That's when we found out about the ingrowing. It's also how we learned what to do with the things you become if you cut your hair. The Injuns told us how to use the swamp bark to knock out and kill one of 'em. Didn't have to torture 'em none to get that information neither.

"After that, they just gave up and told us everything we wanted to know. We got them to perform a ceremony that put us in control of the whole place. They assured us that it would belong to me and Bill, but mostly Bill, for all eternity. Or, as they put it, for as long as the sun shines, the grass grows and the rivers flow. That's what Bill was talking about when he said he'd had assurances.

"They also performed a rite putting the ol' Injun and the young brave in our power, so they would serve us and keep the Eternal Dreaming intact for as long as their bloodline existed. The ol' Injun died but the young brave grew up to be that wily bastard Rivers Flow. We corrupted him over time, and he got to like the power and the money Dead Scalp brought him. Dead Scalp was what we renamed the place.

"Course Rivers Flow got too greedy in the end and that's what undid him. Maybe it was that young Mexican spitfire he took in, I hear she developed rich tastes. Anyway, he tried to rip off Bill and that cost him his two young sons. He started muttering about getting even with Bill for a while, but he soon forgot about that."

Clem drained the last of the whiskey. It hit the back of his throat and he breathed it in. Great wracking coughs burst from his chest as his body tried to get the whiskey out of his lungs. Each hack and splutter set off explosions inside his cranium. Stars burst behind the eyelids he'd squeezed tight.

Clem kept his eyelids shut as the searing, harrowing pain took over his head. murdered every thought inside it and took hold of his senses. Clem realized there wasn't much point holding on to life, if this was all he had to look forward to. Death was better than this torture and disfigurement.

He'd lost his taste for life anyway. The monotony and the drudge of life in Dead Scalp had worn him down. Nothing ever changed. Everything lost its flavor. The joy and the thrill of life were slowly sucked out of a man. Even gambling and sex became pointless. He may as well be dead. At least he'd cheat the blasted hair.

He travelled through the red mist of pain into an endless, numb blackness. Like the Eternal Dreaming, Clem knew that this was a place from which he'd never return.

This realization brought him more relief than he'd known in his entire life.

# CHAPTER 10

James watched as Clem quit coughing, dropped the bottle and stopped breathing. He hoped Bill wouldn't blame him for Clem's death.

He stood and peered out from behind the closed shutters. Nothing moved on the central street except for the hair that was growing up the sides of the buildings, including the saloon. James and Bill could very well be the last two people alive.

Bill burst back in through the connecting door. His arms were full of carved stones, a couple of weird looking rattles and a brazier. Bill dumped all this on his desk and glanced over at Clem. "'S'matter with him?"

"He died, I'm sorry, I know he was your friend."

Bill was quiet for a moment and stared hard at the floor. He seemed to be choking back his grief, so as not to show any type of weakness in front of another man. James was cautious enough not to say a word. Finally, Bill nodded and seemed to come back to himself.

Bill swept all the papers and other objects from his desk. "Gimme a hand with this."

He arranged the brazier and other objects in a careful pattern. Before James could do anything, both windows exploded inwards and the shutters were torn from their hinges.

James wheeled round to see a tide of hair pouring through the windows and over the floor. James lunged for one of the sabers. Bill scrabbled with some matches and swamp bark.

James slashed at the hair which moved out of his way, then wrapped itself around both his wrists. He was yanked off his feet and pulled back towards the wall, where the hair pinned him with his hands above his head. Bill had also been pinned to the wall with his hands over his head before he could light any bark.

More and more hair pushed its way into the room. The loose strands began to interweave themselves, creating complex plaits. The plaits formed themselves into two columns that looked like legs and feet. Then the legs continued to grow upwards, weaving a torso and then a head and two arms complete with hands.

The figure that now stood before them looked like a wise, elderly Injun woven entirely out of hair. The figure crossed its arms and stared implacably at Big Bill.

Bill narrowed his eyes and smiled a cold humorless smile. James could see he recognized the figure that stood before them.

"Tsiishch'ili, you redskin, sumbitch. What in hell do you think you're doing here?"

The figure spoke in a voice like a thousand knotted strands of hair being brushed. "William Baldwin, weren't you just about to summon me?"

"Only to kick your red ass back to whatever hell I sent it to!"

"It would seem to me that I'm not the one who is currently in hell."

"Is that why you're doing this? Trying to destroy my town. You want to send us all to hell, huh?"

"I'm not the one who's responsible for this."

"Oh really? Well, forgive me for asking just who the fuck *is* responsible, if it's not you? See, this hair comes from the graveyard where we stuck your corpse. So it's already got your stink all over it."

"Are you still so ignorant of what's really happening? Have you not known all along why only hair grows here? This is a part of the dreaming world. The hair is your dreams made manifest. It is simply your worst nightmares given substance. Your subconscious fears of retribution finally surfacing. I'm not even Tsiishch'ili, just a guilty memory that lurks in your subconscious."

"Don't try and wriggle out of this. You swore to me, when you did the ceremony and handed this place over. It would all belong to me as long as the sun shines, the grass grows and the rivers flow!"

"This is a land outside of time and space. No rivers flow here and no grass grows either, that's not even the sun shining in the sky. While we're talking of swearing, do you not recall that you swore you would let us all live? But the moment the ceremony was over you butchered me and my fellow shamans."

"We did what we had to. I ain't about to apologize. We brought some order to this place. We brought trade and we brought commerce. We found all kinds of ways to exploit what you were wasting and we got rich off the back of it. It don't belong to you savages anymore. This is American territory. You can't have it back no matter how much hair you send."

"As I said, William Baldwin, this is not hair. These are your dreams, breaking through the soil. This is your American dream, rising up to choke you, as you always knew it would."

"We had a deal!"

"Which you broke when you severed the bloodline and killed Rivers Flow's children."

"We didn't sever shit. That old Redskin can have more brats any time. We might have killed his kids but we didn't kill Rivers Flow and that's what counts. The bloodline is still intact. We're still anchored to the outside world. The deal still stands. You can't be here. Now get the hell out of my town before I choke you with your own guts all over again."

"Ah yes, I'm very glad you mentioned that. It makes this so much more poetic."

The figure of Tsiishch'ili unfolded his arms and pointed at Bill. His arm unraveled itself and the loose strands shot towards Bill's face. Bill struggled, tossing his head backwards and forwards, but the hairs forced his jaws apart and a whole trunk of them plunged down his throat.

Blood trickled from the corner of Bill's mouth. His legs went into spasms and he beat his palms against the wall, cracking the wood. His head bent backwards and the hair began to withdraw.

Bill grabbed instinctively at the trunk of hair, but he couldn't stop it as it left his throat and tore his intestines out of his mouth. Blood dripped down Bill's chin as his lower colon was yanked from between his dislocated jaws.

James saw Bill blink with disbelief, as the hair wrapped his intestines around his neck and pulled them tight. Bill's face went from red to purple. It swelled up with the pressure and his eyeballs bulged so much in their sockets, that James was afraid they would pop out of his head.

James could hardly believe that Bill was still alive, let alone filled with righteous indignation that the Injuns had dared to cross him. He went to his death believing Dead Scalp still belonged to him according to the terms of the agreement.

James knew that wasn't the case. He also knew now why the old devil he'd got the silver dollars from, was so easy to rob.

Everyone had said it couldn't be done, that the place had too many men and was too well guarded, but James was desperate and up against it. He needed the ten thousand entry fee so bad, he was prepared to rob Dead Scalp itself. To make off with the money they kept on the outside, under Rivers Flow's watchful eye. It seemed kind of fitting to use Dead Scalp's own money to buy his way into the place. So long as they didn't find out, he'd have nothing to worry about.

Rivers Flow had put up no fight as James filled his saddle bags. Then he'd accompanied him to the plateau and performed the ceremony to open the portal, just like James told him.

At the last minute, just as the portal was about to open, Rivers Flow had grabbed the saddle bags and made a dash for it. James had chased him behind a big boulder nearby. He was much older than James and couldn't run as fast.

James had knocked him to the ground, but Rivers Flow wouldn't give up the saddlebags. So James had taken the knife from his boot and plunged it into the old devil's heart.

James had been wiping the blood off his knife as the portal opened. James hadn't been too bothered about this, with Rivers Flow gone there were no loose ends. What bothered him was why Rivers Flow had smiled as James pushed the knife between his ribs. Why he seemed so satisfied.

As the hair closed in on him James knew at last. When he killed Rivers Flow, James had severed the bloodline and sentenced everyone in Dead Scalp to death, before he'd even entered. Rivers Flow had smiled because he'd finally got his revenge on Big Bill for the murder of his sons.

The hair swarmed over James like a final revelation. He knew that no sun would shine, no grass would grow and no rivers would flow for anyone in Dead Scalp ever again.

THERE YOU HAVE IT, PARDNERS. THE DREAM OF DEAD SCALP IS OVER AND DONE. AS DEAD AS JAME'S DREAMS OF ESCAPING THE LAW.
AS DEAD AS THE BLOODLINE THAT HELD IT TO THIS WORLD. SOMETIMES, OUR BEST EFFORTS TO EVADE FATE ARE THE VERY THINGS THAT BRINGS US DOWN. AND FOR SOME OF US, REVENGE IS A DISH THAT'S BEST SERVED FROM BEYOND THE GRAVE. JUST ASK RIVERS FLOW.
TRUST YOUR UNCLE JASP ON THIS, YOU KNOW IT MAKES SENSE.

# ABOUT THE AUTHOR

Multiple award-winning author **Jasper Bark** is infectious—and there's no known cure. If you're reading this you're already contaminated. The symptoms will manifest any time soon. There's nothing you can do about it. There's no itching or unfortunate rashes, but you'll become obsessed with his mind-bending books. From the acclaimed *Draw You In* trilogy and the groundbreaking *Bark Bites Horror* series, to graphic novels like *Bloodfellas* and *Beyond Lovecraft*.

Then you'll want to tell everyone else about his visionary horror fiction. About its originality, its wild imagination and how it takes you to the edge of your sanity. We're afraid there's no way to avoid this. These words contain a power you're hopeless to resist. You're already in their thrall, you know you are. You're itching to read all of Jasper's bloodstained books. Don't fight this urge, embrace it. You've been bitten by the Bark bug and you love it!

# JOIN JASPER'S CULT

Would you like to read four more of Jasper's books absolutely free?

Of course you would. Who doesn't like free books?

Jasper's infamous novella, *Stuck On You*, is now free to own as soon as you join Jasper's cult and sign up to his mailing list with this link:

**https://mailchi.mp/jasperbark/jasper-bark-email-sign-up**

Don't worry—you won't have to shave your head or unalive any celebrities (for the first couple of years). But you will get all of Jasper's latest, videos, podcasts, blogs, breaking news on upcoming books, and other crucial information to help you cyberstalk him.

What's more, you'll get two more short novels, a graphic novel and a spoof picture book, just to sweeten the deal! That's five free books just for signing up. These books are exclusive to this offer. You won't get them anywhere else.

Are we crazy? Of course we're crazy! We're asking you to join Jasper's cult!

And because we know you can't bear to miss out, here's that link again:

**https://mailchi.mp/jasperbark/jasper-bark-email-sign-up**

# THE END?

**Not if you want to dive into more of Crystal Lake Publishing's Tales from the Darkest Depths!**

Check out our amazing website and online store or download our latest catalog here.
https://geni.us/CLPCatalog

We always have great new projects and content on the website to dive into, as well as a newsletter, behind the scenes options, social media platforms, our own dark fiction shared-world series and our very own webstore. Our webstore even has categories specifically for KU books, non-fiction, anthologies, and of course more novels and novellas.

Readers…

Thank you for reading *Dead Scalp*. We hope you enjoyed this novella. If you have a moment, please review *Dead Scalp* at the store where you bought it.

Help other readers by telling them why you enjoyed this book. No need to write an in-depth discussion. Even a single sentence will be greatly appreciated. Reviews go a long way to helping a book sell, and is great for an author's career. It'll also help us to continue publishing quality books.

Thank you again for taking the time to journey with Crystal Lake Publishing. You will find links to all our social media platforms on our Linktree page.
https://linktr.ee/CrystalLakePublishing

Follow us on Amazon:

# MISSION STATEMENT

Since its founding in August 2012, Crystal Lake has quickly become one of the world's leading publishers of Dark Fiction and Horror books. In 2023, Crystal Lake officially transitioned into an entertainment company, joining several other divisions, genres, and imprints, including Torrid Waters, Crystal Lake Comics, Crystal Lake Games, Crystal Lake Kids, and many more.

While we strive to present only the highest quality fiction and entertainment, we also endeavour to support authors along their writing journey. We offer our time and experience in non-fiction projects, as well as author mentoring and services, at competitive prices.

With several Bram Stoker Award wins and many other wins and nominations (including the HWA's Specialty Press Award), Crystal Lake Publishing puts integrity, honor, and respect at the forefront of our publishing operations.

We strive for each book and outreach program we spearhead to not only entertain and touch or comment on issues that affect our readers, but also to strengthen and support the Dark Fiction field and its authors.

Not only do we find and publish authors we believe are destined for greatness, but we strive to work with men and women who endeavour to be decent human beings who care more for others than themselves, while still being hard working, driven, and passionate artists and storytellers.

Crystal Lake Publishing is and will always be a beacon of what passion and dedication, combined with overwhelming teamwork and respect, can accomplish. We endeavour to know each and every one of our readers, while building personal relationships with our authors, reviewers, bloggers, podcasters, bookstores, and libraries.

We will be as trustworthy, forthright, and transparent as any business can be, while also keeping most of the headaches away from our authors, since it's our job to solve the problems so they can stay in a creative mind. Which of course also means paying our authors.

We do not just publish books, we present to you worlds within your world, doors within your mind, from talented authors who sacrifice so much for a moment of your time.

There are some amazing small presses out there, and through collaboration and open forums we will continue to support other presses in the goal of helping authors and showing the world what quality small presses are capable of accomplishing. No one wins when a small press goes down, so we will always be there to support hardworking, legitimate presses and their authors. We don't see Crystal Lake as the best press out there, but we will always strive to be the best, strive to be the most interactive and grateful, and even blessed press around. No matter what happens over time, we will also take our mission very seriously while appreciating where we are and enjoying the journey.

What do we offer our authors that they can't do for themselves through self-publishing?

We are big supporters of self-publishing (especially hybrid publishing), if done with care, patience, and planning. However, not every author has the time or inclination to do market research, advertise, and set up book launch strategies. Although a lot of authors are successful in doing it all, strong small presses will always be there for the authors who just want to do what they do best: write.

What we offer is experience, industry knowledge, contacts and trust built up over years. And due to our strong brand and trusting fanbase, every Crystal Lake Publishing book comes with weight of respect. In time our fans begin to trust our judgment and will try a new author purely based on our support of said author.

With each launch we strive to fine-tune our approach, learn from our mistakes, and increase our reach. We continue to assure our authors that we're here for them and that we'll carry the weight of the launch and dealing with third parties while they focus on their strengths—be it writing, interviews, blogs, signings, etc.

We also offer several mentoring packages to authors that include knowledge and skills they can use in both traditional and self-publishing endeavours.

We look forward to launching many new careers.

This is what we believe in. What we stand for. This will be our legacy.

Welcome to Crystal Lake Publishing—Where Stories Come Alive!